ALL YOUR REASONS

Nina Levine

USA Today Bestselling Author

Book 1 in the Crave Series

*Dear Nikki,
Everyone needs
a Jett !
Nina
Levine
xx*

Dear Nikki!

Enjoy your read!

Editing by Editing4Indies
Cover Design ©2015 by Romantic Book Affair Designs

Chapter One
Presley

As I take the call I've been waiting six months for, the people around me carry on with their lives as mine stands still. It's funny how that happens. How, in the blink of an eye, your life can change so completely and yet everyone else is unaware. If they were to look at you, they wouldn't know anything had changed.

I'm in the middle of running a photography shoot, and I've got people everywhere. In amongst the noise and chaos, my world is being tilted, and I'm struggling to focus on what's being said.

"Presley, are you listening to me?"

His question pulls me back into the conversation. "It's too late now, Lennon. I needed you to say this to me six months ago."

He sighs and it's as familiar as an old cardigan. It's the same sigh he's used on me numerous times throughout our marriage, the sigh that tells me how frustrated he is with whatever I am asking of him. "How can it be too late? We've been married for three years, that's not something you just give up on. I want you back, and I'll do anything to make that happen."

The pain his words inflict tears another hole in my heart. "The reason it's too late is because you should have been willing to do anything to make our marriage work while we were in it or when I told you there was a problem. But you didn't. You were too busy with your work to care about me and telling me six months later is not enough. You need to accept this is over and move on."

"That's not gonna happen, baby. You're mine and I'm coming home to show you how wrong I was."

"You're coming back to Australia?"

"That's what I just said. I'll be there next week. Once we finish up with the tour."

Now it's my turn to sigh. He just doesn't get it. "And that's why we'll never work," I say softly.

I know him so well I can almost hear his brain thinking and I can picture his brows pulled together in confusion as he asks, "Why?"

"Because if you truly loved me and wanted me back, you wouldn't be waiting for the bloody tour to end." I take a breath before adding, "Don't come back, Lennon. I don't want to see you." I bite my lip as I prepare to end the call.

Darla, my assistant, is watching me closely, and she raises her brows, questioning if I'm okay. She knows the last thing I need on this shoot is for my concentration to be challenged. And she can probably tell from my body language and facial expressions that's exactly what's happening. She's worked with me for a long time and been my friend for longer. She knows me well. I nod at her to indicate I'll be okay, because I will be. This isn't the first time my husband has screwed with my

6

concentration. I'm well versed in dealing with it and getting through my work, in spite of it.

Lennon's patience gives way. I'm surprised he's lasted this long with that short fuse of his. "Presley, you don't know what you want half the time," he snaps. "We're meant to be, and you'll see that when I get there."

"Goodbye, Lennon," I say and hang up because otherwise we could be going back and forth all day. He just doesn't listen. I knew it while we were together, but since we broke up, it's become even clearer to me.

Darla approaches. "You okay, boss?"

"That was Lennon," I say.

Her eyes widen. "What did he want?"

"Apparently, after all this time, he's decided he wants me back. Says he's coming home in a week or so to show me how much."

"That bloody asshole!" She's never been a huge fan, not after she saw the way he always put our marriage second to his career.

"I feel like this truly is the end now, you know?" I don't know why I feel sad about this all of a sudden. I've spent the last six months trying to get over him, and I've started moving on, but after that conversation, it feels more final. I look at Darla with resignation. "I don't know, maybe deep down I still hoped he'd come and fight for me, but what he's doing doesn't feel like enough. Does that sound stupid?"

She madly shakes her head. "No, it doesn't, and you're right . . . this is all too little, too late."

I slowly nod. "Yeah, it is."

We stand in silence for a moment, both lost in thought about the demise of my marriage. Eventually, Darla claps her hands together. "Okay, back to work. We're going to get this shoot finished and then we're gonna go out and get drunk."

I shake my head and grin mischievously at her. "No, you might be going to get drunk... I'm going to get laid."

Laughing, she agrees, "Yes, you are. And I might just do that, too."

***

I finish applying lipstick to my lips, place it back in my purse, and then run my fingers through my long, blonde hair, messing it up as I go. The straight hair trend shits me to tears;

8

give me messy, wild hair any day over that perfect, boring look. Stepping back from the mirror, I assess my outfit for tonight; skintight black leather pants, heels, and a slinky red sleeveless top. I've finished it off with an assortment of bracelets and my silver Tiffany heart tag necklace. *Yeah*, I grin, *tonight I'm going to score.*

"Presley, babe, you made it."

I divert my attention from the mirror to the voice behind me. Shit, I'd forgotten she'd be here tonight. Jade Garcia. Supermodel. Shallow bitch from hell. *God, give me strength.*

Before I can reply, her food deprived friend interrupts. "You're the photographer from today's shoot, aren't you?"

Full points to the vapid supermodel wannabe. I bite my tongue on so many witty remarks and instead, simply reply, "Yes." Well, okay, perhaps they weren't witty, so much as catty. I can be one of the cattiest bitches you'll ever meet. That could be why I don't have a lot of friends. That and the fact that I truly dislike most people I meet.

Jade starts gushing to her friend. "Presley is one of the best photographers I've ever worked with. They had to pay a small fortune to get her to work on this shoot."

I tune her out; I've heard it all before, and I'm over it. I'm also over working with models and clients with no imagination. This shoot bored me to fucking tears, and I won't be in a hurry to work with them again.

"I've got to meet another friend, Jade. I'll see you around," I say as I begin to make my way out of the ladies' room.

She raises her eyebrows. "A Valentine's date?"

"God, no!"

"You don't like Valentine's Day?"

"What's there to like? A commercialised day that puts pressure on people to buy shit that supposedly proves how much they love their partner. I've never celebrated it and don't ever plan to," I reply, noting her stunned expression.

"Wow. I've never met a woman who doesn't love Valentine's Day." Her previous awe of me has been replaced with disdain. If I'd known it would be this easy to change her opinion of me, I would have shared my thoughts earlier.

I shrug. "Well, now you have. Love's an everyday experience; it's something shown in the mundane things you do for your partner. It's not found in a fucking overpriced bunch of flowers picked up on the way home from work because you know if you don't get them that day, of all days, your life won't be worth living."

Jade's eyes are glazing over; I probably lost her at mundane.

"I'll catch you later," I say as I push open the door and exit the room, not waiting for her response. With a bit of luck, I'll never have to see her again.

The cool air of the club hits my face and I welcome it after the heated stuffiness of the crowded ladies' room. It's Friday night and pumping in here. Everyone is celebrating the end of the work week. I'm celebrating the beginning of my holidays. Three months of no work. Three months of doing whatever the hell I want. *Bliss.*

I make my way to the bar and order a bourbon and Coke. After slamming it down in two gulps, I motion to the bartender to pour me another.

"Hard day, sweetheart?"

Turning to see who is speaking to me, I am momentarily speechless while I take in piercing blue eyes and gorgeous features. Whoever this man is, he has the ability to turn me on just by being near me because I am turned way the fuck on right now. As electricity sparks through me, I imagine running my hands through his dark hair and laying kisses along that chiseled jaw. Need and desire swirl together and I decide that he will be mine tonight.

"Hard week, more like it," I answer him just as the bartender brings me another drink. Before I can get cash out of my purse to pay for the drink, the guy lifts his chin at the bartender, who nods and walks away without taking payment. I'm still trying to find cash in my purse and the guy puts his hand over mine, stilling it.

"Why was your week so bad?" he asks, his hand still on mine.

I move my hand away. "Thanks for the drink."

He flashes me a smile that shoots more electricity through me. "You're very welcome. Now tell me about your week."

I sigh. "I'd rather not talk about it. Let's just say that dealing with pretentious, self-centred people for twelve hours a day, five days in a row, is enough to make me consider moving in with the Amish and adopting their way of life."

He chuckles. "I hear you. It sounds like we've been dealing with similar people all week."

I cock my eyebrow. "Oh, no. I fucking win this one, dude. I've been working with models who couldn't work out their left from their right half the time."

He nods, another smile forms on his face that would melt my panties if they weren't already melted. "You win. I could think of nothing worse than working with models."

My gaze sweeps over him, taking in his jeans and black t-shirt that both hug his body. He's rocking muscles I am fighting not to drool over; muscles I need to hold my hands back from because all they want to do is touch. Those muscles are covered in tats, and I squint to try and read what one of them says. It looks like a quote written in cursive on his forearm, but I struggle to work out what it says.

He sees me looking and holds his arm out as he tells me what it says. "Fate loves the fearless."

I grab hold of his arm and position it so I can read it better. The moment I touch him, I feel it, and I know he feels it, too, because his eyes show it. There's an undeniable spark between us, and as soon as it hits me, my body lights up at the thought of sleeping with him.

As I let go of him, he leans his face close to mine and asks, "You feel that?"

Not letting go of his eyes, I nod. The slow burn of desire is eliciting a hunger in me I haven't felt for a long time. And I sense he wants me just as much as I want him. "I do," I finally answer him, slightly breathless.

The beat of the music surrounds us, and the crowd threatens to drown us, but I am lost to the moment and almost unaware of everything else as we search each other's eyes. I'm sure I detect warmth and kindness in his. Odd that I'm getting all that when I've just met him, but I would swear it on a bible.

He slowly moves his face away from mine and drinks some of his drink. As he places the glass back on the bar, he says, "I'm Jett."

14

"Presley."

A smile tugs at his lips. "Your parents are Elvis fans?"

"My mother is and my father is blinded by love. She could have called me Elvis and he wouldn't have blinked."

This inspires a laugh out of him. "Your parents are still happily married?"

"Yeah, go figure. How many marriages do you know of that are still going strong after thirty years?"

His eyes twinkle. "My parents are still happy after thirty-five years. I guess you and I are like some weird science experiment. It kinda sucks, really."

Frowning, I ask, "Why?"

He throws the rest of his drink back, his eyes still twinkling. "When you don't come from a fucked-up family, you can hardly blame your issues on your parents, can you? Nope, you and me, we have to own our fucking issues."

I burst out laughing. "You are so right. Shit, pass me my drink, I can't cope with this knowledge."

Shaking his head, he holds my drink away from me. "Bad idea, sweetheart. You have no one to blame your alcoholism on except yourself. I suggest you give up alcohol straight away and find a new vice that's not as socially unacceptable as alcohol addiction."

Oh, this is fun. I raise my eyebrows. "What do you suggest?"

He doesn't even hesitate. "Sex addiction. Take that shit up. Much easier to hide from public view. And a lot more fucking fun than dealing with hangovers."

"I wouldn't know the first thing about taking that up. You think you could help me with that?"

He pulls a face like it's the hardest question he's ever been asked. Nodding, he says, "Sure. You want to get started now?"

My core clenches at the thought, and I lean into him and say, "You've no idea how much I want to get started on that now, Jett."

He sucks in a breath, and his hand curls around my neck. "You sure? Because once I'm finished with you, you're going to have an addiction that will be hard to kick."

"I'm more than sure. But if my newfound addiction gets out of hand, you might have to step up and help me break it."

"Oh baby, I can't think of one good reason to break that kind of addiction. No, I'll just step up and feed it. Can't have you fighting cravings, can we?"

Now it's my turn to suck in a breath. "Jett, it's fun to stand here and flirt with you, but I've gotta say, I'd rather you take me back to my hotel and fuck me."

He grins. "I thought you'd never ask."

Grabbing my hand, he begins to lead me away from the bar but I pull back and stop him. When he gives me a questioning look, I say, "I need to let my friend know I'm leaving."

"Sure."

I dial Darla. She's in this club somewhere, but I haven't seen her for a good hour. A couple of moments later, after I've spoken to her, Jett and I leave the club. I'm barely containing myself; I haven't been this excited for sex in a long time.

***

Thank god the hotel I'm staying at is close because Jett can't keep his hands off me and I'm about to explode with desire. We stumble through the door to my room and he pushes me up against the wall before pressing his lips to mine in a searing kiss. He tastes so good. I could spend hours devouring his lips and mouth. When his tongue tangles with mine, I moan and thread my hands through his hair. He groans and grinds his erection against me.

He breaks our kiss and cradles my face with his hands. His eyes search mine, and he murmurs, "Fuck, you're beautiful. How the hell are you not already taken?"

I run my finger over his lips. "Maybe I'm too much of a handful for just one man."

"Perhaps whoever tried wasn't enough of a man to know how to handle you right."

I grin at him and pull his face back to mine. Brushing my lips over his, I say, "I get the feeling you're a smooth talker, Jett."

A laugh escapes his mouth, and his eyes crinkle as he smiles. "I've been accused of that before, sweetheart, but don't let it turn you off." He moves to whisper in my ear. "I'd really like to help get you started on your new addiction."

As he moves his face back away from mine, I say, "I don't give a fuck if you're a smooth talker. Sweet-talk me all you like, so long as you back it up with an orgasm or two."

He quirks an eyebrow. "Only two?"

"Well, feel free to give me more. I won't complain." I give him a wink and then reach for his belt and undo it. A moment later, I've got his jeans undone and am stroking his cock while watching his eyes close with pleasure.

"Fuck...feels good," he groans.

I bend and take him in my mouth. This man is well endowed, and I'm consumed with lust. Usually I like to draw sex out, make it last, but tonight I'm rushing to the finish line. I need him inside me. Now.

As my desire takes over, I stand, push his jeans down and rip his shirt off. His eyes snap open as he kicks his jeans to the side. "Someone's eager," he murmurs.

I'm not even slowing down. My top is off faster than he can blink, and my shoes and pants follow soon after. And then I'm standing before him in my underwear, almost panting with need. I trail my fingers down his chest, taking in the tattoos covering his body. There's hardly an inch of him not tattooed, and as much as I'd love to stand here discovering

19

what they all are, I don't have time for that tonight. No, tonight is all about getting as many orgasms out of him as possible. "We're in for a long night," I promise.

"I'm down with that."

"I thought you might be."

He reaches out and slips his hand inside my bra, pushing the cup aside so my breast is exposed. His thumb rubs my nipple, and a moment later, his mouth is on me, sucking, licking and gently biting. As he pushes the other cup out of the way so he is holding both my breasts, he asks, "You know what they call women with tits like yours?"

"No, enlighten me."

Looking up at me, he says, "Dangerous."

"Really? That's the best you've got?"

Straightening so his face is close to mine, he slides one hand around my neck and grips me there while his other hand cups my cheek and his thumb rubs over my lips. He brings his lips to mine and lightly kisses me. When he speaks, his voice is growly and sends delicious sensations to my core. "Really. Tits like these have been known to make a man do stupid things. We lose all fucking reason when we see them, and to hold and taste them, well fuck, that just sends us over the edge, sweetheart." He pauses and his eyes hold mine for a moment. They're speaking to me, silently. They're flashing desire and telling me how much he wants me. "Pretty fucking dangerous," he adds before leaning in to kiss me again.

I'm consumed by his kiss and his need. I have the same need. As he kisses me, I push his boxers down and then move my hands to take my panties off, but he has other ideas, and his hands are on mine, stopping them. I break the kiss and give him a questioning look. "You don't want them off?"

"I do, but I will have that honour," he answers me and then hooks his fingers in my panties and begins to slowly pull them down.

I watch in pleasure as he begins to lay kisses down my body and then kneel in front of me. He removes my panties and then stills, taking me in. His eyes on my pussy do amazing things to me, and I tingle with anticipation. If his eyes can do that, I know I'm in for a hell of a treat when he gives me his mouth.

When he takes his first taste of me, I sway a little, and his strong hands grip my legs, steadying me. He holds me as he runs his tongue from one end of my pussy to the other, and it's a good thing he does because I'm experiencing a heady rush of hunger. I'm not sure my legs would hold me up without his help. And then he pushes his tongue inside and my mind explodes with light and my body pulses with ecstasy.

I grip his hair and moan. Wild lust courses through me. I can hardly hold myself together as he works his magic with his tongue, and I know it won't take long for him to bring me to orgasm. His hands glide up my legs to hold my ass, and as he grips me there, it's almost like he's trying to pull me closer to him. It's not possible, though; Jett has his face buried in my pussy as deep as he can. He's got talents a woman can only dream of and I'm disappointed this will only be a one-night stand. I'd like to sample these talents again.

When he stops what he's doing, I want to push his face back to me. I'm about to beg him to keep going when he asks, "Do you have any idea how fucking good you taste?"

"No, but I'll believe you so long as you keep tasting me."

His eyes remain on mine as he begins to massage my clit with his finger. "I wasn't sure if you might prefer my finger to my tongue."

Oh good god, he's going to drive me insane with lust. "That's a hard choice. Maybe you should decide."

His eyes sparkle with mischievous delight. "Mmmm . . . let me see." His finger is inside me a second later, and I close my eyes as I let the sensations wash over me. "Feel good?" he asks.

I nod because seriously, I can't even form a thought at this point, let alone a word.

"Good," he murmurs, and then he replaces his finger with his tongue.

"Fuck . . . Jett . . . don't fucking stop," I moan, my eyes still closed, my hand gripping his hair.

And then he takes me on a ride I never want to get off. His tongue and his fingers work together to bring me to orgasm. When it hits, I realise I've been missing something in my life. Jett gives me an orgasm like I've never had, and I scream his name as I shatter into a million fucking pieces of bliss.

My legs give way again, and he swiftly moves to stand up and hold me. As his arms go

23

around me, his lips crash down on mine, and he kisses me into blissful oblivion. I am completely consumed with this man; tonight, he is owning my mind and body in a way no man ever has. And we've only just gotten started.

When he ends the kiss, I open my eyes to look into his. He's watching me with a look I can't quite put my finger on but I ignore it and say, "You think my tits are dangerous? I think your mouth is."

He laughs and murmurs, "Wait till you have my cock, sweetheart. I promised you an addiction you'll struggle to break, and I always keep my promises."

"Can't wait," I whisper, the effects of my orgasm still messing with my ability to form thoughts.

"Neither can I," he says, letting me go. His eyes wander down to my bra, and he reaches behind me and flicks it undone in one easy movement. "I'm not sure one night with these tits will be enough," he says as he slides my bra off. He lets it drop to the floor and bends to kiss my breasts again. The passion he kisses them with tells me he really can't get enough and that turns me on even more than I already am.

I reach for his cock and grasp it firmly before I begin to move my hand up and down his hard length. His breathing picks up and he stops what he's doing and straightens. Smiling at him, I bend to take his cock in my mouth.

The minute I wrap my lips around him, his hand lands on my head and he groans. "Fuck, Presley..."

And then my phone rings.

I ignore it and keep sucking him. No way am I letting anyone interrupt us tonight.

"You wanna get that?" he asks, although I can tell he doesn't want me to.

I swirl my tongue over him, and he sucks in a breath. "No. Whoever it is can wait 'cause I've got more important things to do."

"Thank Christ," he mutters as his eyes flutter shut.

My phone stops ringing but then starts again.

Bloody hell.

We both continue to ignore it, but when it rings a fourth time, I swear and let him go.

"Sorry, I'll tell them to fuck off and be right back."

He rakes his hand through his hair, frustrated, and smacks me on the ass. "Hurry up, my dick fucking needs your mouth."

I love his dirty talk and answer my phone begrudgingly. "What?" I snap without even looking to see who it is.

"I've hurt my fucking ankle." It's Darla. *Shit.* I can tell from her voice she's in a great deal of pain.

"Where are you, hon?"

"I'm in my hotel room, just got back, but I tripped in the bloody gutter and twisted it. Are you able to come to my room and check it out? I don't think it's broken, but I need a second opinion."

My gaze shifts to Jett's hard on. *Fuck.*

He catches my gaze and gives me a questioning look. I frown and give my attention back to Darla. "Sure, I'll be there in a minute."

She sighs. "Thanks, babe."

"Of course," I say and hang up. There's no way I can let my friend down in her hour of need. She's been there for me every step of the

26

way through my marriage break-up, and although I have an aching need for Jett to fuck me, Darla always comes first.

"You're leaving?" he asks, but there's no anger there.

"Yeah, sorry. My friend's twisted her ankle, and I want to make sure she hasn't broken it." The regret is clear in my voice.

"Shit," he says and begins to get dressed. "I'll come with you."

"What?"

"I'll organise for someone to pick her up and take her to the hospital so you don't have to worry about it. You can just take care of her while I sort this out for you."

Mind blown.

"Thank you, I appreciate it," I murmur, surprised at his offer. I'm more surprised at the way he's handling this, though. If I'd stopped mid blow job with my ex to run off and check on a twisted ankle, he'd have been pissed and wouldn't have hesitated to let me know.

"No worries."

We get dressed and then head to Darla's room. As we wait for her to answer her door, I say, "Sorry about this."

27

He grins. "It's all good, but you owe me and I'll be collecting."

Hell yes. I return his grin. "I like the way you think."

Before he can say anything else, Darla answers the door and I take in her distressed state. Mascara is running down her cheeks, along with tears. Darla never cries so I know this is bad. I take one look at her ankle and suspect she's broken it. "Shit, Darla, that looks nasty." I usher her to a chair and then dial down to the front desk and request for ice to be brought up to her room.

I'm so engrossed in helping her, I forget to introduce Jett so he does it for me. "Hi, I'm Jett."

She smiles through her tears. "Goddamn, you scored well," she says to me with a wink.

Jett laughs, not even slightly thrown by her remark. I get the feeling he's heard this before. "It's good to - "

Darla cuts him off. Her eyes have widened and she looks like she's about to hyperventilate. "Oh my god, you're Jett fucking Vaughn!"

"Who?" I ask, taking in her excitement and his blank look.

She's excited, but the pain has taken over again, and she can't answer me, so I look at Jett who is watching me with another look I can't read. Usually I'm good at reading people, but this is the second time tonight I've not been able to read him.

He scrubs a hand over his face. "You didn't know, did you?"

My brows knit. "Know what? I have no idea what either of you are talking about."

"Fuck," he mutters.

"Are you going to tell me?" I ask, wishing one of them would fill me in.

Darla's pain subsides enough for her to answer me. "He's the lead singer of Crave." That means nothing to me, and when she realises that, she exclaims, "God, Presley, how can you not know who Crave is? They're one of the best known rock bands in the world. You of all people should know who they are."

Jett steps in. "Not everyone has heard of us, Darla. I do occasionally find someone who doesn't know me."

She rolls her eyes. "Well, now you're just being humble. Everyone knows who you are."

She gives me a pointed stare. "Except Presley which is odd because - "

I cut her off. "I don't know every rock star in the world." I give her a dirty look and then look at Jett. "Sorry."

He shakes his head. "No, I loved that you didn't know."

I send him a wicked grin. "I'm not into rock stars so we can just pretend I don't know."

He chuckles. "You're on." And then his phone rings and he turns away to take the call.

Turning my attention back to Darla, I bend down and ask, "How are you feeling, hon?"

Her face is etched with pain. "I've never been in so much pain. Do you think it's broken?"

"I have no clue. Jett's organising a car to come pick you up and take you to the hospital."

She looks at him in awe and then gives me a dreamy grin. "He's got a good reputation, you know. Goes through women, apparently, but a nice guy regardless. It's so nice of him to do this for me."

"Oh god, you know that most of the shit you hear in the press is crap so I don't know why you listen to that rubbish."

She shrugs. "It's Jett Vaughn, babe. I've been following him for years. I can't believe I've met him, but bloody hell, why did it have to be when I look like shit?" She pauses before her eyes light up again and she adds, "Fuck, I can't believe *he's* your one-night stand."

I laugh and wink at her. "Yeah, he's the guy I had my lips wrapped around when you rang."

"How the hell did you get so lucky?"

I'm just about to answer her when Jett comes back. "Sorry to interrupt, ladies, but I've got a car waiting downstairs for us." He looks at Darla. "I'll carry you down if you'd like."

I'm sure she's about to burst from either pain or excitement and I would bet good money on the latter.

She's tiny, and he easily carries her to the car. Me? I'm still in shock this man gave up a blow job to take my friend to the hospital.

CRAVE

Chapter Two
Jett

I lean against the wall in Darla's hotel room and watch Presley look after her friend. God, she's beautiful. I've met some stunning women in my life, but Presley has that something else to go with her beauty. And that shit puts her above the stunners with no personality. Watching her now, I see kindness and compassion, and it stops me dead in my tracks because it's not often I come across those anymore. Most of the women I meet these days are fairly shallow, and while I'll fuck them, I don't want to spend any time with them.

Presley's different. I've known her for less than six hours, and I'm already planning our next three dates.

We got back from the hospital half an hour ago. Darla hasn't broken her ankle. It's just a bad sprain so they sent her back here with drugs and instructions for rest and ice.

She leaves Darla, who is almost asleep, and walks to me. "It's late, Jett. You should go get some sleep."

"Aren't you forgetting something?"

She frowns. "What?"

I bend to whisper in her ear. "Your lips. My dick."

I hear her suck in her breath and know she's keen but her eyes betray her tiredness. "Oh, that," she murmurs. And then her tummy grumbles.

Cupping her chin, I ask, "You hungry?"

A small smile pulls at her lips and she puts her hand to her stomach. "Yeah."

I nod. "Okay, let's go get you something to eat."

"It's nearly three am. I'm sure you must have stuff planned for today. Don't you want to get some sleep?"

I grab her hand. "What I want to do is feed you, sweetheart. Sleep can wait."

She covers the surprise I see on her face with a grin and squeezes my hand. "I know your game, dude. You just want to get me fed so I'll have the energy to finish that blow job."

I stifle my laugh so I don't wake her friend. Dragging her out of the room, I ask, "How is it you know me so well after such a short amount of time?"

"Men... you're all the same. If there are lips on offer, you'll do almost anything."

"Guilty as charged."

"So, where are you taking me?"

"I know a little café that's open all night. They make the most amazing food."

"Oh god, don't tell me that. I'm trying to lose some weight at the moment, and amazing food is the last thing I need. I don't know how to stop when the food is that good," she complains.

I eye her petite frame. She's got curves, but there's no way in hell she needs to be on a fucking diet. Scowling, I say, "Do you have any clue how sexy you are? Those curves of yours are every man's fucking dream."

Her eyes widen and I'm stunned to think I've told her something she should have already known. Something any man in his right mind would tell her. "There's always room for improvement," she says quietly, and I want to take a match to those thoughts and burn them from her mind.

I shake my head. "Not for you." I yank her hand and pull her to me. Her body collides with mine, and the heat between us flares. Running my finger along her lips, I say, "As far as I'm concerned, your sexiness is off the fucking charts. Don't change a thing."

A smile eases onto her face. "Every woman needs a Jett. You could singlehandedly fix the mental health of most of the women I know."

I steal a kiss and then smack her ass. That ass is one I could happily spend hours getting to know and laying my hand on it is something I want to do more of. Pulling away, I boss her around. "Okay, start walking. Food heaven awaits."

***

Ten minutes later, we arrive at the café and the owner gives me a huge smile. I've been coming here on and off for five years, so they know me well. He gets us settled and takes our order. I'm pleased to see Presley order up big. After the owner leaves us, I say, "I take it you don't live here due to the fact you're staying in a hotel. Where are you from?"

"Brisbane. You?"

Inside, I'm cheering like a dickhead. "Brisbane, too."

"Are you here for work?"

"Yeah, we came to Sydney to do some concerts." I shift in my seat and lean across the table a little. "You said you were working with models. What do you do?"

"I'm a fashion photographer. However, I'm thinking of swapping to landscape photography," she says, and I note the sarcasm.

I chuckle. "Had enough of the models?"

"You have no idea. I've been working in this industry for seven years, and I think I've hit my used by date."

"So, time for a change?"

She nods, clearly enthusiastic about this idea. "I've got three months off, and I'm going to reassess everything."

I cock my head. "Sounds like you're about to make a lot of changes, not just work."

"Yeah, it's been one of those years, you know?"

"I do. Although for me, it's been *more* than one of those years." Exhaustion pounces on me just thinking about it.

"Oh god, that sucks," she says, and I'm in complete agreement with her.

"Yeah, it does, because I love making music. It's just all the other bullshit that goes with it that I hate."

"Which part?"

"I miss my family and friends. When we started the band ten years ago, I never cared about being away from them, but over the last few years, I've really started resenting it. In fact, we're just about to take some extended time off, something we haven't done for a long time," I say, taking in her surprise. "Why do you seem surprised?"

"I'm more impressed than surprised," she says, softly.

"Why?"

"I've met a lot of famous people through my work and other things, even made friends with some of them, and they hardly ever talk about their family. You've mentioned yours twice already tonight. So yeah, I'm surprised but impressed."

A sensation I've never felt snakes through me. I'm clueless as to what it is, but I soak it in. It's the kind of sensation I would pay good money to feel more of. "I know what you mean, sweetheart," I murmur.

"Do all your band members get on well?"

"Ten years is a long time to work together and practically live together. We've hardly stopped touring in that time. But I'm pretty proud to admit we work at it and do get on fairly well still. There have been some bumpy parts, though. I guess it's like a marriage."

"You've been married?" she asks, seemingly interested in my answer.

"Fuck, no. Besides the fact I haven't met the right woman, I wouldn't like to put a marriage through my job. I don't know what I'll do if I ever get married, but I'm fairly certain I'd cut my work back."

And there's that surprised look on her face again as she says, "Like I said, every woman needs a Jett. Do you know how many friends I have who would kill to have a husband who put them before their work?"

"You know, I'm kinda liking this whole 'everyone needs a Jett' thing you've got going on but only so long as it's you who wants a Jett and so long as it's for more of the lips-on-dick action." I give her a wicked grin, and she shakes her head in amusement.

It's refreshing to find a woman with a great sense of humour. As we start laughing, our food arrives and we spend the next hour eating and talking. It's easy, which is something rare for me. I find most women difficult to talk to. All they want to do is screw me and worm their way into my life by blinding me with sex. I'll take the sex any day, but what I crave is good conversation and some laughs. So far, Presley has managed both.

She gives me a serious look when we finish eating, and says, "I think you'd better take me back to the hotel now if we're going to have any hope at finishing what we started. Otherwise, I may fall asleep mid sex."

Without hesitating, I stand and reach for her hand. "Let's get going then," I say as I assess her. It's obviously been a long week for her because she looks exhausted.

It takes us longer to walk back than it did to get here, and I'm beginning to wonder if I should just carry her, but she makes it on her own. When we enter her room, I pull her to me and kiss her. She kisses me back but there's even exhaustion in her kiss. I figured that would be the case, and as I end the kiss, I smooth my hand over her hair and murmur, "Let's get you to bed."

She looks puzzled. "Don't you want to have sex? My lips, your dick . . . remember?"

"Beautiful, you have no idea how much I want to fuck you, but I'm thinking that in your current state even my dick won't keep you awake."

A tired smile graces her gorgeous face and she nods. "You're probably right."

She walks to the bed and grabs the t-shirt that's under the pillow. I expect her to change in the bathroom, but instead, she strips down to her panties and pulls the t-shirt on. Fuck, her body is spectacular with its curves and a softness I don't see on many women. I don't even pretend not to watch. No, I settle my ass against the table in the corner, fold my arms across my chest, and enjoy the fuck out of the show. Not that she's turning it into a show, but Presley undressing *is* a fucking show.

Once she's changed, she pulls the bed covers back and gets in. I move to the bed and pull them over her before squatting so we're at the same level. I want to take one last look at her before leaving. Her eyes are already closing and she smiles at me as she fights sleep.

"I'm so glad I went to that club tonight," I admit.

The smile is still on her face and her voice is sleepy. "I'm glad you went, too."

"When do you fly home?"

"Tomorrow, late afternoon." She's barely awake now.

"I want to see you again, Presley."

"Yes . . . the sex will be good . . . we need to do that . . . "

"No, I want to take you on a date."

"No dates . . . just sex . . . I don't do rock stars . . . " she mumbles through a sleepy haze.

"What do you mean you don't do rock stars?"

"No, don't want to do it again . . . "

She's almost asleep, and I have no clue what she's talking about, so I decide to finish this conversation when she's awake. I kiss her on the forehead and stand. "Night, sweetheart."

There's no response except for her steady breathing as she sleeps. She looks so peaceful. I consider sitting in the chair and watching her for a while, but it feels wrong, so I don't do it. Instead, I take one last look at her and then leave. This won't be the last time I see her. She can try to say no to me all she likes, but I'm not the kind of man who ever takes no for an answer. If I want something, I always find a way to have it.

Chapter Three
Presley

I hang up the phone from Darla and mutter a swear word. Our flight has been cancelled, and while she's decided to take the opportunity to stay in Sydney for a couple of extra days, I have to get home. My cat, Urban, has been staying with a friend, and I need to get back to him. I'm just about to call the airline when there's a knock at my door.

"Hi," I say, surprised to see Jett.

He holds a coffee out to me and takes a step forward to enter my room. Although I'm not sure I want him here, there's a sureness in his stride I like. "Morning." He greets me with a million dollar smile that sets butterflies off in my stomach.

Shit.

"To what do I owe the pleasure?" I inquire as I take a sip of coffee. Hot damn, it's good coffee. Just what I need this morning.

He walks further into the room before stopping and turning to face me. "Just checking in on you. You were pretty tired so I wanted to make sure you didn't miss your flight."

"Thank you." I hold the coffee up. "And thank you for this. It's heaven in a cup."

"It is, isn't it? It's from that same café I took you to."

"I'll have to remember that café the next time I visit Sydney."

"What time's your flight?"

"It's been cancelled, so I'm just about to find a new one."

A thoughtful look crosses his face. "I have a spare seat you can take."

"Huh?"

"My band's flying home at seven tonight, and our manager was supposed to fly out with us, but he has to stay another night now, so we have a spare seat."

I'm not sure why I'm feeling all mushy and excited at his suggestion when my head is screaming to refuse. I don't fucking do mushy. And yet, my heart and stomach are all mushy.

Shit.

The words fall out of my mouth before I can stop them. "That would be great."

His face lights up. "I'll organise it. We're leaving the hotel at four, though. Sorry about that."

"I don't mind, but why so early?"

He sighs. "Our drummer, Hunter, has this thing about always being on time. He hates being late, and we always have to leave for everything hours in advance."

I shrug because I get that. Totally. It's something I do. "Well, I guess on the upside, your band must have a reputation for never being late to a concert. I bet your fans love you for it 'cause I've gotta say, there's nothing worse than when you go to a concert and they can't even be bothered to start on time."

He grins again. "Yeah, that's us, and you're right, the fans do love it. Thank fuck for Hunter, huh?"

I raise my coffee in the air. "Cheers to Hunter."

He chuckles, and it warms me. It's been too long between men for me, and I'm enjoying this more than I want to. "I would ask you to lunch, but I've got some meetings to attend before we head out."

I wave my hand at him. "No, that's okay. I've got editing to do anyway. I'll see you at four down in the lobby."

He spends a moment or two looking at me. I'm not sure why, and it flusters me a little. And the fact it flusters me, shits me because I don't get flustered. A bit like I don't do mushy. Bloody hell, this man is bringing all kinds of shit out in me.

I'm relieved when he finally speaks. "Okay, sweetheart. I'll see you then."

He leaves, and I'm left in a bewildered state. It's been a long time since a man's managed that. I'm a little disappointed, though. Jett's a rock star and I won't date a rock star ever again. Not after the last one ripped my heart out and left me to bleed tears of heartbreak and regret.

***

I spot Jett as soon as I enter the lobby later that day. He's standing near some couches, talking on his phone. Sitting on the couches are three men and they all look fairly bored. Must be his band members.

As I walk over to them, Jett spots me and grins. By the time I get to them, he's ended his call and gives me his full attention. "You still look tired. You didn't get to catch up on some sleep?"

"No, I had to get my editing done. Did you get any?"

He shakes his head. "No, we've been in meetings all afternoon."

His band members are all watching me with what looks to be fascination. One of them stands and comes toward us. The grin on his gorgeous face is devious, and I wonder what he plans to say. I rake my gaze over him. He's tall and muscly, but not in an overly built way. It's what I call a skinny-muscly look. His dark hair looks good against his tanned skin, and he's rocking some serious ink, even more so than Jett. I don't have any tats, but the artist in me loves the idea of decorating my body with meaningful images and words.

"I can see why Jett gave you our spare seat," he says, appreciative eyes checking me out.

"I see you aren't the only smooth talker in your band," I say to Jett.

He grimaces. "Yeah, meet West, he likes to think he's smooth."

West shrugs, a lazy grin on his face. "There are a lot of women out there who would agree with me."

"Yeah, well, unless you want to lose a nut, keep your eyes to yourself," Jett threatens.

Another one of the band members comes over and introduces himself. "Hi, I'm Hunter, the only sane member of this group," he says with a friendly smile. If I didn't know he was in a band, I possibly wouldn't have suspected it. He seems almost shy and doesn't have the standard rock star look going. Instead, he has the gorgeous blonde hair, blue eye look that makes him look quite wholesome. I don't tend to go for blondes, but he's gorgeous. And while

I can't see any visible tattoos or piercings on him, I wonder what he's got hidden under his clothes.

I return his smile. "So, what you're saying is that I should run now, right?"

He laughs, and it lights up his face. Oh god, I bet he has the women falling at his feet. "Nah, Jett's cool. He loses the plot sometimes, but other than that, he's a good guy. It's Van you need to worry about the most out of all of us. He's a crazy motherfucker. Best to steer clear."

Van is still lounging on the couch, watching and listening. He doesn't get up; rather he just gives me a chin jerk and mutters a greeting I can hardly hear. I nod back, not sure what to make of him. He's dressed in leather pants, a t-shirt, and chains around his neck – your typical rocker outfit. And he seems to have the attitude to go with it.

"How in the hell did you meet this asshole?" West asks.

"He bought me a drink and then told me I needed a new addiction. Let's just say the conversation was fascinating."

"A new addiction? What the fuck?" West was looking between Jett and me for an explanation.

Jett grins but doesn't say anything so I enlighten him. "He suggested I give up alcohol and take up sex. Much easier to hide a sex addiction."

West bursts out laughing. "That's fucking classic, man. You seriously score chicks with that shit?"

"He seriously did," I say.

"Fuck!" West is clearly impressed, and I feel the need to clarify something.

"That line wouldn't work for just anyone, though. It worked for me because the minute I saw Jett, I wanted to sleep with him, so pretty much whatever line he came out with would have worked."

"Every woman he meets wants to sleep with him. Fucking lead singers get all the chicks," West grumbles.

"She didn't know who I was," Jett joins in the conversation.

West is floored, Hunter looks stunned, and even Van leans forward to hear more.

"What the fuck?" West finally mutters.

Jett remains silent, leaving it for me to explain. "Sorry guys, but I've never heard of you before now. I don't really keep up with bands. If I like a song, I'll check it out, but even then, I don't tend to remember the name of who sang it."

Hunter's mouth has fallen open. I think I've really shocked him. "What kind of music do you like?" he asks me.

"I love country. I could listen to that all day. But I do like some rock, just not the heavier stuff."

"Do you know the names of anyone you like?" he asks.

"Yeah, I like Florida Georgia Line, Carrie Underwood, Blake Shelton . . ." My mind goes blank for a moment before I exclaim, "Oh, and Keith Urban, I love his stuff."

"That'd be fucking right, nearly every woman I meet has it bad for him," West mutters, clearly annoyed at the love for Keith.

I grin. "Dude, you can see why, right? I mean, if you were a woman, you'd give it up for him, too."

"Not fucking likely." He scowls at me.

Jett steps in. "Just ignore West, he's only got a thing against Keith because a girl he was trying to score years ago ditched him to chase after Keith." Looking at West, he says, "You need to let that shit go."

While Jett and West are rehashing old times, Van stands and motions towards the front door. "Get your shit together, guys. The limo's here." He picks up his bag and heads outside without waiting for anyone else. I have no idea what to make of him. Perhaps he's just tired from work, and once he catches up on sleep, he'll be more sociable. Mind you, he *is* a rock star and they can be moody bastards. I should know.

***

I do up my buckle and sneak a look at Jett. He's watching, though, and catches me, sending a huge grin as he does. I shake my head and grin back at him. Ever since I met him in the lobby hours ago, he's been flirting with me. It's been the best three hours of my life in a long time.

52

He moves his face to mine and whispers, "I'm not a member of the mile high club yet, sweetheart. You want to initiate me?"

Desire is almost exploding out of me after all his flirting, and his request threatens to send me over the edge. I don't want to date another rock star, but I won't say no to sleeping with this one. I place my hand on his leg and begin tracing a pattern on the inside of it, knowing full well the effect this will have. When he sucks in a breath, I know I've achieved my goal. "No, I can wait till we get back to Brisbane. I need more room than that to do all the things I want to do."

"Fuck," he hisses. "Do you have any fucking idea what you're doing to me right now?"

"A little," I admit sweetly.

He removes my hand from his leg and places it back in my lap. "If you keep that shit up, my dick will embarrass all of us, baby."

I try not to laugh but can't contain it. "Really? A rock star who gets embarrassed about that kind of stuff?"

He groans. "Can we just forget I'm a rock star? And yes, my mother taught me better than that."

I like his mother without even meeting her. "Mmmm . . . a rock star with manners. I like that."

"Manners in public but none in the bedroom," he promises, his warm breath against my ear.

I turn my head slightly to make eye contact. "I like that even better."

"Yeah, you will."

His voice has turned all growly and lust is blazing from every inch of his body. He's turning me way the hell on, so in an effort to get us under control, I change the subject. "Why doesn't your band have a private jet?" We weren't mobbed at the airport, but the band did attract a lot of attention, and their security had to work hard to keep the crowd away.

"When we're in the States, we travel that way, but we don't really see the need in Australia."

"So you're bigger over there?"

He seems uncomfortable discussing this, and in a way, that impresses me. I like that he doesn't want to talk about this, that he doesn't want to talk himself up. "Yeah, we do have a lot of fans over there."

"Fair enough."

"I've got a question for you now. Why don't you date rock stars?"

I shift in my chair and look down at my hands before looking back up at him. "I just don't."

"Yeah, but why? What do you have against us?"

"Jett, I don't have anything against you personally, but I'm not interested in dating someone who is too busy with their work for me."

"Well, you're in luck then. I'm about to have plenty of time for dating." He flashes me another smile. Jett's smiles are irresistible. They make me want to forget my scars of hurt and let him in.

"How about we take it one step at a time."

"I'm all for that, sweetheart. One date at a time."

I lean into him. "I was thinking more like we finish what we started last night and go from there."

"If you're trying to get out of a date, it's not going to work. First we fuck, and then I take you out for dinner. No ifs or buts."

"You're very demanding, aren't you?"

"I get what I want, Presley, and I want a date with you."

I know I'm not going to win this round. He's just too damn persistent. So, I plaster a smile on my face and agree. "Okay, but you better perform, otherwise there's no date."

He laughs. "Performing is what I do best, beautiful."

God help me.

***

I unlock my front door and pull Jett inside. His flirting on the plane and the drive here has been relentless, and I'm desperate to get our clothes off and have him inside me. He's worked me into such a state, I don't think he'll actually have to do very much at all to give me an orgasm. His words alone are orgasm inducing.

We make it into my bedroom, clothes almost all discarded, and he wraps his arms around me, holding me close. His mouth descends onto mine and we lose ourselves in a kiss that tells each of us how much we're wanted. He's fucking me with his mouth, and I'm sure my pussy would reach out and grab hold of his dick if it could.

"I need you in me now, Jett." I talk while kissing, so I'm not sure if he'll understand what I'm saying, but he does.

He pushes his erection into me, and it's a torturous bliss. Ending the kiss, he growls, "I fucking need that too, sweetheart."

The only piece of clothing separating us is my panties, and he rips them off. Literally rips them in half. Then he picks me up and throws me on the bed. Feral desire flashes in his eyes as he climbs on top. He straddles me and holds out a condom. I have no idea when he got that, but I'm more than impressed we don't have to fuck around any longer. If he doesn't get his dick in me soon, I'm going to go crazy.

I take the condom and have it on him in record time. Shifting my gaze to his, I beg, "For the love of god, fuck me."

He doesn't say anything, just grunts his approval and positions his cock at my entrance.

His lips smash down onto mine, and as his tongue enters my mouth, he thrusts inside.

Oh . . . holy fuck . . . shit . . . fuck!

My arms go around him, and I dig my fingers into his back as I take everything he gives me. Jett fucks me with a raw need. I feel it flowing between us, connecting with my same need. It joins us and we move in perfect synchrony. Sex has never felt this good for me and I have an overwhelming desire to give him more than I've ever given a man. A desire to open myself up completely and let him take anything he wants from me.

He stops moving and looks at me with hunger. "You wanna ride me?"

I do, but not now. Now, I just want him to fuck me until I see nothing but exploding light. I shake my head and squeeze my legs around him tighter. "No."

No more words are needed and he thrusts inside again. He does it slower this time while holding himself above me and keeping his eyes pinned to mine. It's like he's trying to look into my soul, like he's searching for something there. His eyes reaching out to me while he fucks me awakens my closed off heart. I'm helpless to stop it, and as he moves me closer toward orgasm, he also moves me closer toward *him*.

"Fuck, Presley, I'm gonna come. You close, baby?" His head drops down to rest on my shoulder as he keeps moving inside me.

"Yeah..." I move with him, chasing it.

And then it hits. White light begins flashing behind my eyes and pleasure like I've never known possesses me. I hold onto him tighter and my core clenches around him.

"Fuck!" he roars as he comes hard. He thrusts one last time and then his body tenses as his release grips him.

I'm lost inside my own pleasure just as much as he's lost in his. We're clinging to each other, but for those few moments, we're disconnected. The only thing we're connected to is our bliss.

Eventually, he lifts his head and murmurs, "Shit . . . "

I open my eyes to look into his. Giving him a smile, I nod my head. "Yeah . . . shit."

He laughs and pushes up off me to go and dispose of the condom in my bathroom. Then he comes back and lies next to me on his back. We're silent for a while, and I love that he doesn't feel the need to fill the silence with small talk.

He reaches for my hand and holds it. "You okay?" he asks.

I'm trying to process all the emotions coursing through me. I truly don't know what I'm feeling. But I turn to him with a smile and shift onto my side. Trailing my hand up his stomach to his chest, I reply, "Yes, I'm more than okay."

He pushes a couple of strands of my hair off my face. "Was that performance good enough to score a date with you?"

God, he has no idea.

"As if you're going to let me say no," I mutter, not wanting to admit to either of us just how much I now want that date.

He chuckles softly. "Good point."

I shift positions onto my back, and we're quiet again for a while. It's not until he presses a kiss to my forehead that I realise I've almost fallen asleep. I blink and look up into his eyes. "Sorry."

His face crinkles into a smile. "All good, sweetheart. You obviously need some sleep, so I might go."

Disappointment washes through me but I say, "Okay."

I mustn't do a very good job at hiding what I'm feeling because he says, "I don't want to go, trust me. But I've got an early morning tomorrow and I really think you just need some sleep without me distracting you. If I stay, you're not gonna get much sleep."

"You're right. I do need sleep."

His eyes search mine, almost like he's making sure I'm being honest. Then he brushes his lips across mine before pushing up off the bed. As he dresses, I also leave the bed to dress so I can walk him out.

At the front door, he snakes his arm around my waist and kisses me. "I'll call you," he promises before turning and leaving.

I trudge back to bed trying to ignore the sinking feeling in my stomach. He says he'll call, but will he? And do I really want him to? I have such warring emotions where Jett is concerned, and I fall asleep with the thought that it'd be best if he didn't because then the decision will be taken away from me. And I won't be able to fuck another thing up in my life.

Chapter Four
Presley

I sink down into the chair at the café and look at my best friend, Erin, sitting across from me. "What?" I ask as she grins at me.

"You've totally been laid."

"I have."

"Tell me more," she throws out as she opens her menu and glances down at it.

"First, tell me if you've heard of a band called Crave."

"Fuck yeah, everyone's heard of Crave."

"Shit." *Am I the only person on the planet who hasn't heard of them?*

"Oh my god, did you fuck one of the Crave men?"

I answer her only with a smile.

"Holy fuck, Presley!" She's momentarily impressed but then she remembers who she's talking to. "Wait, I thought you were done with rockers."

My chest heaves, and I blow out a long breath. "I was . . . I am . . . " My voice trails off as I struggle with this answer.

"Oh god, you're not."

I take in her concern. Erin watched me fall apart while Lennon treated our marriage as if it meant nothing to him. "Jett seems different."

Her eyes widen. "Jett Vaughn . . . bloody hell, you attract them, don't you?"

"What does that mean?"

"Jett's the ultimate rock star, sister. He fucks 'em and leaves 'em. Don't do this to yourself."

I bite my lip. "I think I'm past the point of no return," I admit.

"Fuck," she mutters. "You do remember you met, fell for, and married Lennon in a matter of four weeks, don't you? And that it wasn't the best decision you ever made."

"Yes, and I'll never do that again. And trust me, I don't want to fall for another rock star, and I've told him that, but there's just something about him I can't say no to."

"Crap," she says, and then she reminds me why she's my best friend. "Well, I guess we're taking a ride on the rock star train again."

I grin at her, relieved she's not giving me a hard time over this. "Have I told you lately that I love you?"

"No, you haven't told me that. You've been so damn busy with your work. And on that, how did your shoot go?"

The waiter interrupts us to take our orders and then I open up to her. "I'm in a rut with my work. It's gotten to the point I don't even want to get up in the morning if I've got a shoot on. Those models are slowly killing my soul, and I don't think I want to take on any more fashion jobs."

"I've been waiting for you to tell me this."

"Really?"

"Yeah, the writing's been on the wall for awhile now. Sounds like you need a timeout."

"Well, I've got my three months off, so I'm going to spend some time really thinking about it."

She nods. "Good. I can't wait to see what you come up with. What's Darla going to do?"

"She's travelling Europe for a couple of months, and then I guess we'll see where we're at. She hurt her ankle while we were away, so she's decided to stay with her family in Sydney for a week or so because she's struggling to walk on it."

"Shit. I hope it gets better before she leaves for Europe."

"You and me both. Now, tell me what you've been up to," I say.

Erin's an accountant and she fills me in on her work and also updates me as to which guys she's currently dating. She always dates more than one guy at a time and is so damn fussy I'm worried she'll grow old alone.

Our food arrives and we laugh about her sexcapades while we eat. Hanging out with Erin is like coming home, and by the end of our lunch date, my soul feels happier. As we're walking out of the café saying our goodbyes, my phone rings.

"It's Michael," I say. "I'd better get it or he'll just keep calling." Michael's my agent and has a tendency to forget people have lives outside of work.

She gives me a hug goodbye. "Keep me updated about Jett," she orders, and I nod.

As she walks away, I answer my phone. "What's up, Michael?"

"Presley, I've got a job for you tonight."

"No, I told you no more jobs for three months, and I meant it."

"I know, but this isn't a fashion job, so I thought it might be a foot in the door to something new."

My interest is piqued. "What is it?"

"Concert photography."

"Michael, I know nothing about concert fucking photography."

"You underestimate yourself, darlin'. And besides, they've asked for you in particular."

"What the hell?"

He ignores me as he usually does. "So, you up for it? Can I tell them yes?"

He's right; a foot in the door is what I need. And besides, doing this job will tell me if this

66

might be something I'm interested in. "Sure, book me in."

"Thank fuck 'cause I already told them yes. They're sending a car for you at five."

"Jesus, why so early? Is this a kid's concert?"

"No, not a kid's concert. Not sure why they want you there so early, but they're paying you good money for this, so just run with it."

"Okay," I say absentmindedly because I'm still wondering why the hell someone would request me for this job.

"Gotta go, babe. Talk to you tomorrow." He hangs up and I realise I never asked him who the band was. Guess I'll have to wait to find out.

***

Five o'clock rolls around and I'm waiting patiently to be picked up. Jett hasn't called, and I hate to admit I'm disappointed. But perhaps when he said he'd call, he meant within the next few days. I'm giving him the benefit of the doubt, even though Erin told me he's a player. I've spent the afternoon trying not to think about him, but I can't get him out of my mind. And it's put me in a bad mood. Not the fact he didn't call, but rather, the fact he's gotten under my skin.

My thoughts are interrupted by a knock on my door. Time to get this show on the road.

As we drive to the venue, butterflies form in my stomach. I've been trying to avoid thinking about how nervous I am, but now that we're nearly there, I can't ignore it any longer. Fuck, I hope I don't let them down. That would definitely *not* be a foot in the door.

Turns out the concert is at the Brisbane Entertainment Centre which only intensifies my nervousness. They must be a successful band to be performing here.

Why the fuck did they request me?

The driver pulls into a closed off carpark and lets me out where I'm greeted by a security guard. I tell him my name, and he radios the information to someone else. A moment later he lets me in, giving me directions as to where to go.

There are people everywhere, all hurrying around me as I head off in the direction he indicated. My phone buzzes with a message, and I pull it out of my bag to check it.

Michael: Kick ass babe xx

Me: Thanks. Will do, otherwise I'm kicking your ass for getting me into this shit.

Michael: I'm leaving town. Didn't I tell you?

Me: All good. I can hunt you down.

I shove my phone back in my bag and am still thinking about Michael a couple of minutes later when I spot a familiar face at the end of the corridor I'm in.

What the hell?

Jett?

I do a double take and realise it really is him. He's watching me with an intensity that sends desire through me. I want him, there's no denying it.

I walk to where he is. "*You* requested me?"

His intense stare doesn't waver as he answers me. "I had to be sure I'd see you again."

I've never had a man look at me the way he does. It's want, need, and hunger all wrapped up in appreciation, and I want to bask in it forever. I never want him to stop looking at me like that. And I sure as hell don't want him to ever look at any other woman like that. Shit, jealousy has reared its ugly head, and I don't even have a reason to be jealous. I'm fucked if I ever do, and if I date him, I'm sure I'll have plenty of reasons.

"Did you think I'd not make good on my promise of a date?"

"Wasn't taking any chances," he murmurs as his eyes shift to look behind me.

"Hey, Presley," a voice behind me says and I turn my head to find Hunter looking at me.

"Hi, Hunter."

"So, you're gonna photograph us tonight, huh?" he says.

"It would seem so," I answer him but move my gaze back to Jett. He's watching me again with that intense look. His body is tense, and he seems to be on edge a little. I'm not sure why.

"Can't wait to see what you come up with." He gives me a warm smile and lifts his chin at Jett before leaving us.

"Do you really want me to take photos?" I ask Jett, unsure of his intentions.

"Hell, yes. I asked around about you and have heard amazing things about your photography."

"Who'd you ask?" I'm keen to know who recommended me.

"I asked a photographer we've worked with before. Shane Nichols. You heard of him?"

"Holy shit! *Shane* recommended me? He's one of my inspirations. I love his work." Jett would have no idea what this information means to me. I'm blown away Shane would recommend me, let alone even know who I am.

"Yeah, he did. He said he's been following your career for awhile now and loves your work. Also said you have a very unique style to your photography."

"You do realise I haven't done concert photography, don't you?"

His intense stare finally gives way to that grin of his I'm beginning to love. "Yeah, but seriously, with what I've heard about your skills, I'm sure you'll come up with some amazing photos."

His belief in me is unexpected but appreciated. Hell, when your own husband didn't have unwavering belief in everything you did, it's almost mind blowing for someone you've just met to show it.

"Thank you," I say softly.

He grabs my hand and begins walking us down the corridor. "Come on, let's get you set up," he says, and my initiation into his world begins.

***

Jett watches me as I survey the stage. We're standing to the side of it where roadies are busy with the finishing touches to get it ready for tonight. "You're nervous about this, aren't you?"

I turn to him. "I'd be lying if I said I wasn't."

"Why?"

"In the photography I specialise in, I have full control over the models, the lighting, and the angles I can shoot." I motion toward the stage. "With this, I have no control over any of that. There's also the clutter to take into account."

He seems fascinated with this. "What do you mean by clutter?"

"Things like microphones, stands, cables, amplifiers, scaffolding in the background, lighting rigs... those sorts of things. And then if I'm photographing, say you, and I have the shot all lined up but then another band member jumps into the shot...that kind of thing is another issue." I smile at him. "Don't get me wrong, I'm really looking forward to this, but I'm nervous I'll let you guys down."

"Presley, I've no doubt you're gonna do a spectacular job. You won't let us down, so please stop worrying about that. Just listening to you talk shows me that you know what the hell you're talking about."

His words calm me a little. My nerves have already started to ease. Having the time to check the stage out and come up with some ideas has helped me with that, and I silently thank Hunter for his compulsive need for everyone to be here hours before the concert begins.

"Jett," a guy calls out from the stage.

He turns to see who is calling for him, nods at the guy, and then looks back at me. "That's our lighting tech, so I need to see what he needs. Are you okay on your own?"

I nod and give him a reassuring smile. "Go. I'm all good."

"Okay, sweetheart. I'll see you backstage after the concert," he promises before jogging to where the lighting tech is waiting for him.

I watch him for a little while. He seems to have a lot of control over how the concert will run, and I've gotten the impression he takes charge of the band a lot. So far, though, I haven't seen any evidence of that being an issue for anyone. They seem to naturally defer to him when a decision needs to be made. I like his take-charge attitude, but the thing I like about it the most is he leads rather than controls. There's nothing worse than being told what to do with little regard for what you want.

***

A couple of hours later, I'm fully into the swing of this. The concert is packed and the energy is electric. Jett and the guys know how to deliver a show, that's for sure. And their fans eat it up. They love the band in a way I've never seen before. I've been to a lot of concerts, but Crave draws the crowd in and makes them feel like old friends. And their music is amazing. I can't believe I've never heard it before. I really do need to get out more.

I started off a little rocky, but I quickly worked out what I was doing. After spending some time watching each band member and learning their idiosyncrasies, I worked out the best shots to aim for. Jett has this way of leaning away from the mic during pauses in songs, so I've managed to capture that pretty well, I think. Van is the lead guitarist, and he and Jett have this chemistry on stage that creates some great photo ops. I've been able to capture their dynamic really well, and I can't wait to see how the photos turn out. And then there's Hunter on the drums and West on rhythm guitar. I got some great shots of the both of them, too, and I'm quietly confident all my photos will turn out well and the guys will be happy with them.

As they wrap the concert up, I take in their fans. It's pretty clear they've loved every minute of it, but at the same time are disappointed it's over. I can relate for a couple of reasons. Number one, I think I've fallen in love with photography all over again, and I could keep going for hours. And number two, there's a backstage party after the concert, and I really don't want to go. Hanging out with groupies is the last thing I want to do.

CRAVE

Chapter Five
Presley

*M*e: *I kicked* ass.

Michael: Knew you fucking would. Thank god my ass is spared.

Me: No your ass is still on the line because now I'm at the after party and these people are nearly as bad as those fucking models I hate.

Michael: Leaving town now...

"What are you laughing at?" Jett asks as he comes up behind me and slides his hands around my waist. They settle on my stomach, and I look down taking that sight in. I like it. A lot.

"I wasn't laughing."

His chin rests on my shoulder and his warm breath feathers against my neck as he speaks, causing a new rush of desire to pool in my stomach. "Not on the outside, but I can tell that something has amused you," he says.

I debate whether to be honest with him and then think to hell with it. I've never censored myself for anyone before, so why start now? "I was just texting my agent and told him I am going to kick his ass for this job."

"You didn't enjoy it?"

"No, I did enjoy it. I just don't care much for the people at your after party. I told him they're almost as bad as the models I've been subjected to for years."

A voice booms from beside me. "Oh yeah, they are." It's West. "I totally agree with you there, babe." I remember the day I met him at the airport. He flirted with me enough to piss Jett off, but even then, I could tell he was only doing it to rile Jett up. I don't know him, but West seems to care for Jett a lot.

Jett's hands tighten around my waist, and he pulls me closer to him. "Don't you have a groupie to entertain, West?" His voice is deep and growly as he asks this, and I can feel his body has tensed up.

"Calm the fuck down, dude. I'm not after your woman, but she's cool to talk to. You think you can handle it if I just talk to her for a bit?"

I bite my lip to stop myself from laughing, and West winks at me.

Jett straightens and he repositions me so I'm pulled tight against his side, his hand firm around my waist. "Yeah, I can handle you talking to her, but seriously, take your fucking eyes off her body."

West shakes his head and pins Jett with a glare. "You've never cared before."

"Yeah, well I care now."

They glare at each other for a few moments and then a scantily-clad woman sidles up to West. She gives me a filthy look as she puts her arm around him. "West, you said you wouldn't be long, but you've been gone for ages. Are you coming back now?" Her voice has that breathy, sexpot tone to it, and I take an instant dislike to her. I don't care what anyone says, women like that give the rest of us a bad name.

West rolls his eyes and removes her arms from his body. "No, I'm busy." He doesn't tell her to leave, but his tone speaks volumes, and she understands it. Scowling at me, she huffs and then saunters off.

"Why is that my fault?" I'm pissed and have to restrain myself from following her to give her a piece of my mind.

West chuckles. "Because you've got my attention and she hasn't. Clearly, it's your fault." He throws a wink in while he says this.

"I like you, West. And that's saying something because I dislike most people," I tell him.

A huge smile spreads across his face. Looking at Jett, he says, "Don't fuck this up, asshole. She likes me, and I like her, which is more than can be said for all the other women you chase."

Jealousy rears its ugly head again. I hate this feeling and am reminded why I said I'd never date a rock star again. The constant state of wondering and worrying your man will stray is something I don't want to have to deal with again.

I can hear the scowl in Jett's voice as he replies, "Fuck off, dickhead, and stop flirting with her."

West holds his hands up in a defensive movement. "I'm out of here." His gaze shifts to the door, and his eyes light up. "Fuck me, I'm gonna tap that tonight," he says and heads off in that direction.

Jett and I turn to see who he's talking about, and I'm impressed to discover West has taste. The woman he mentioned has a classy look to her rather than the slutty, groupie look.

I swivel in Jett's embrace so I'm looking up at him. Smiling, I say, "West seems like a cool guy."

The scowl is gone from his face. "Yeah, he's like a brother to me."

"So, all that stuff about him flirting with me was just mucking around?"

"Mostly."

"What does that mean, Jett? I don't want to come between friends."

He pulls me tighter to him. "You won't come between friends, but West has this tendency to flirt with every woman he meets, and if he keeps that shit up with you, he and I will have a problem."

I'm surprised by his words. We've known each other for less than three days, and from what I've worked out, Jett doesn't date. So, I'm left wondering why he's gone all territorial over me.

"Jett!" Van, the other guitarist in the band is stalking towards us with a foul look on his face.

"Fuck," Jett mutters under his breath.

Van stops in front of us, his hard stare focused on Jett. "What the fuck is this fundraising dinner you've agreed to?"

"It's to raise funds for cancer research. I thought you'd be all over it after what your mother went through." His voice is tight, controlled.

"Yeah, but why the fuck would you sign us up for it when you know full fucking well who else is going to be there? I told you I never want to see that motherfucker again."

Van is radiating anger, his green eyes flashing with wild intensity. He's all edge and jaggedness, and I've seen the women flock to him tonight. Van's pure rock star with his dark, shaggy hair, piercings, tattoos, and couldn't-give-a-fuck aura.

"When I signed us up, I didn't know who would be there, and we can't back out now."

Van looks ready to explode with his anger and rakes a hand through his hair. "Fuck!" He turns and takes a couple of steps away from us before looking back at Jett. "If shit goes down there, it's not my fucking fault," he declares and then stalks out of the room.

"Fucking hell," Jett mutters and lets me go. He rubs the back of his neck, and I don't say a word because it's clear he needs a moment. Once he gets himself under control, he says, "Sorry about that."

"No need to apologise."

The air is still tense around us as he calms down. Then he grasps my elbow and begins walking us to the door. "I need to get out of here," he says more to himself than to me, and I follow wordlessly. I have no problem with leaving this party. I didn't even want to be here in the first place.

As we pass through the door, people slap Jett on the back and say goodbye. He's not interested, though, and doesn't respond to any of them. His intent to get us out of here fast is obvious.

He stalks through the corridors and leads us outside to a waiting limo. Without a word exchanged, he indicates for me to get in and I do. He still seems a little worked up about his run-in with Van.

As he settles on the seat next to me, he leans back and drops his head onto the headrest. Pushing out a long, heavy breath, he says, "Jesus, I could do without some of this shit today."

"You wanna talk about it?"

Angling his head to look at me, he replies, "Not really." His hand slides around my neck and he murmurs, "I just want to kiss you and get inside you again. You good with that?"

I nod and he doesn't give me a chance to say anything before his lips come down on mine. I moan into his mouth. His kiss delivers bliss as if it's being injected straight into my bloodstream. The effect is intoxicating, and I want a never-ending supply of his drug.

He ends the kiss and pulls away so he can watch as he slides his hand up my top to cup my breast. His eyes shift to mine, and our gazes stay connected while his hand pushes my bra cup aside so he can tweak my nipple. When his entire hand covers my breast, I feel it in my core. His gaze is still focused on mine, and that alone is enough to cause want and need to spiral through me.

Oh god, I have to have him now.

I move so I'm straddling him, and press my lips to his. I kiss my desire into his mouth, and he groans as I press my pussy against him. He's so hard, and I can't wait any longer for him. I pull away and breathe out, "Condom?"

He reaches into his pocket for his wallet and gives me a condom. "You gonna fuck me, sweetheart?"

I rip the foil packet open and unzip him. There's no time to waste, and I have his cock in my hand a second later and roll the condom on. "Yeah, baby," I say as I strip my pants and panties off. And then I straddle him again and push myself down onto him. He sucks in a breath as he fills me, and I watch as his eyes flutter shut in pleasure.

"Feel good?" I ask as I move up and down his length. If it feels as good for him as it does for me, we're both in for a good time.

His eyes open to look at me. "Yeah," he grunts and then moves his hands so one grips my neck and the other takes a hold of my hair. Pulling my hair, he commands on a growl, "Don't fucking stop. Your pussy is like paradise on fucking crack."

His dirty words work me up even more, and I fuck him with a relentless pace. We're both chasing this, needing the release. Sweat slicks our skin as we careen towards heaven. As it starts to hit, I bend my head and bite his shoulder, swallowing the scream I can't deny.

"Fuck!" He bucks underneath me and comes. His head leans against my shoulder as he surrenders to it.

I ride it out, wringing every last drop of what he's giving me. When I'm done, I sag against him, exhausted. We stay like that for a while until he eventually lifts his head and says, "Fuck me, Presley, you know how to fuck."

"You sure know how to compliment a girl," I tease him.

"Just calling it like I see it." He winks at me and lightly slaps my ass. "Where are we at with that addiction of yours? Have I fulfilled that promise yet?"

I kiss him before giving my answer. "What do you think?"

That wicked grin of his lights up his face. "I'd say we're doing a damn good job of it, sweetheart. But just to be sure, we'd better keep at it."

I grin back at him, which is so unlike me. It seems with Jett, I do all the things I never do with anyone else. "I think we should."

And just like that, it's settled. I'm going to let Jett have his way with my body all night. I'm going to put all my hesitations about him out of my mind and enjoy all the pleasure he gives me.

CRAVE

Chapter Six
Presley

I wake up to sunlight streaming in the window, the rays fanning out across me on the bed.

Jett's bed.

We ended up here after the concert, and he spent hours worshipping my body. I didn't get a good look at his apartment as he was so intent on ripping my clothes off and getting me into his bed, but from what I could see, it's modern and sleek. He doesn't have a lot of personal touches like photos, paintings, and plants, so it's not the kind of apartment I would live in. I wonder how often he's home, though, to even notice.

Rolling over, I find him on his back, still asleep. This is the perfect opportunity to admire his beauty, and I let my gaze roam over his body. His abs are perfectly chiseled and I wonder how many hours he has to spend in the gym to achieve that. And his V? Fuck me, I've never seen one so defined and so fucking delicious. I trace my fingers lightly down it, and he makes me jump when he growls, "You better be ready for me to fuck you if you're gonna do shit like that, sweetheart."

For someone who was asleep, he moves pretty bloody quickly, and in an instant, he's pushed me onto my back and is on top of me. He stares down at me, and says, "Morning." His voice is sleep husky, and I want to bottle that shit. It's sexy and I want to play it over and over in my head for hours.

"Morning," I almost whisper, still distracted by his voice and those muscles. *Oh . . . those muscles.*

He bends his face to mine and softly kisses me. It's a wake-up kiss, but I know it'll quickly progress into something more. The sizzle between us is undeniable, and I doubt we could ever be in the same room without wanting each other.

He deepens our kiss, and I don't even care about morning breath. I want this man and nothing could get in the way of that at the moment. My legs wrap around his body, and I push myself towards him, but he pulls away and murmurs, "Wait a sec, beautiful. I need to wrap it."

Fuck, he's right, and I'm grateful one of us is thinking straight. I watch as he moves effortlessly off the bed and into the bathroom in search of a condom. A moment later, he returns, condom in place.

As he moves over me, he asks, "Now, where were we?"

I loop my hands around his neck and press my lips to his. "Right here."

He spends some time blessing my lips with his, and then begins to trail kisses down my body, stopping momentarily at my breasts before continuing down. His destination is clear, and when he finally gets there, he takes a moment to look at me. Then he shifts his gaze to mine and asks, "Do you have any idea how much I want to lock myself away with your pussy for hours on end?"

Oh, good lord.

"Show me," I say, because truthfully I can't focus enough to form more words than that. Jett has seen to that.

A growl rumbles out of his chest, and he buries his face in me. Warm breath. A tongue that knows what it's doing. A mouth I want to beg to never stop. And I know there's nowhere else I'd rather be. I throw my arms out to the side and grip the sheet as my back arches up off the bed. I'm thinking this kind of pleasure can't be legal when he pushes his finger inside me and brings me closer to the edge. And it doesn't take him long to tip me over that edge.

"Oh, my god, Jett . . . " I can't even finish that sentence; the pleasure he's giving me is so intense it's all I can focus on.

He finishes bringing me to orgasm and then moves on top of me again. I love the wild look in his eyes. That look tells me just how much he wants me, and the feeling this knowledge induces is toe curling. He kisses me – a long, deep kiss – and I taste myself in his mouth.

"See how fucking good you taste?" He's staring at me intently, waiting for my reply.

I nod and bite my lip. His gaze drops to my lips, and he mutters, "Fuck."

He kisses me again and presses himself against me, his cock hitting my entrance. I wrap my legs around him and encourage him in. Jett doesn't need to be told twice; he thrusts in, hard and fast, on a grunt. I swallow a scream and show him how much I want him with my kiss. He fucks me like a man possessed, and I'm sure I now know what nirvana is.

Nirvana is Jett.

His head drops while he pursues his release, and I shut my eyes as it takes over me again. Ecstasy like I've never known wraps itself around my body, curling into me, reaching deep inside, and setting off a chain reaction of sensations that light every single nerve ending of mine with pleasure.

Jett is ecstasy.

I drift off in a sex haze, and it's not until Jett speaks that I come back to consciousness. "You good, sweetheart?"

I open my eyes and look up into his. "Yeah," I say, lazily.

He smiles at me before asking, "You wanna have a shower with me?"

"I don't think I can stand just yet. You go ahead. I'll have one after you, when I've got my legs back."

His smile spreads out into a full-on grin as he pushes up off me. "Addiction complete," he says with a wink and saunters into the bathroom.

I watch his sexy ass until I can't see it any longer and then let out a long breath.

What the fuck am I doing?

I don't want Jett, and yet I want nothing *but* Jett.

Shit.

I need to get my head together. He's a player, so chances are he just wants a short-term thing here. He probably just wants sex. I can do that. I just need to keep my heart out of it because Erin's right; I do tend to fall fast and hard.

Fuck.

***

After I finish showering, Jett surprises me with a request. "Are you free today to photograph a party?"

"What kind of party?" I really just want to go home, lock myself away, and regroup. Being around him causes me to make choices I don't want to make. Choices that are leading me further down the path towards spending more time with him.

His usual sexy grin is replaced with a serious look. "It's a birthday party for a kid who has cancer. We're his favourite band, and he requested us to sing at it. Photos weren't a part of the deal, but I think it'd be cool for him to have them."

My heart melts a little at his generosity and kindness. *Damn, that wasn't supposed to happen.*

"I'm kind of busy -"

He steps into my space, snakes his arm around my waist, and pulls me close. "I know what you're doing," he whispers.

I feel tongue-tied. This never happens; men don't cause me to struggle with my words. "What am I doing?" I manage to get out.

94

"You're trying to avoid me. But see, the thing is, I'm your new addiction, so you *can't* avoid me."

Oh god, if only he knew.

"Is this how you charm all the women you sleep with?"

"I don't charm the women I sleep with. I've never wanted to be an addiction for any of them. You're the first," he admits, stunning me.

"So this is just sex, right?"

"No."

"But what if that's all I want?"

"Sometimes you can't have what you want, Presley." His voice is low, commanding. I hate it, but I love it more. It turns me on, and I resent the desire I have for him to use it more often.

"You're kidding, aren't you?"

His stare is challenging me to argue, like he gets the final say in this. "No. I told you what I want, and I'm going to get what I want."

I try to push out of his embrace, but he tightens his hold on me. "You know you want this as much as I do," he asserts.

"I know I want the sex as much as you do, but you're wrong if you think I want to date you."

His eyes narrow on me, and he relents, letting me go. "We'll start with the sex, but you still owe me at least one date."

"Uh-uh, we had that last night."

"You working at my concert is hardly a date."

"There was a party involved; that's a date in my books." I know I'm pushing him, but I need to. I need to protect my heart.

He shakes his head and mutters, "You're going to test me, aren't you, sweetheart?"

"Not if you understand we'll never be more than sex."

He chooses to ignore that and moves on. "So, about this party today. Are you really busy?"

"Yes." I'm not backing down; it's not what I do, and I'm not starting now.

Nodding slowly, he murmurs, "I'll let you get away with that this once." His voice is quiet but firm. There's a warning in it, and I don't miss it. He's not going to be easy to persuade

to my way of thinking, and I'm not sure if I'm
annoyed by that or quietly excited.

Chapter Seven
Jett

I *scan through* the photos on the computer in front of me. West can hardly hold his excitement in. "Fuck man, she's fucking talented. These photos are the best we've ever had taken."

He's right. The photos Presley took at our concert last week have a quality to them I've not seen before. She's captured atmosphere and emotion, and mixed her own brand of edginess in to create photos any band would kill to have.

"We have to book her for our next tour," Hunter interjects.

Thank fuck our next tour isn't for at least six months, maybe more. I've spent the last week and a half chasing the fuck out of Presley, only to have her foil all my attempts. Either she's busy or she's tired or some other fucking excuse. If I'm gonna convince her to come on the road with us, I might need a full six months to do that.

Van's chair scrapes against the floor as he pushes it back and stands. Putting his aviators on, he says, "Right, that's settled. Book her." Without a backwards glance, he strides out of the room.

"What the fuck is his problem?" West demands, watching Van with a filthy glare. There's no love lost between those two. I spend half my time sorting out their issues, and I'm way fucking over doing that.

"He's pissed about the fundraising dinner I signed us up for," I admit.

"Christ, we've known about that for over a week now. He needs to get the fuck over it," West mutters.

"Yeah, well you two need to get over whatever shit you've got going on. I'm sick to fucking death of dealing with your crap." I blow out a long, frustrated breath.

West scowls at me, but I ignore it. I couldn't give a shit if he's pissed at me. Least of my fucking problems.

Hunter can't handle confrontation and tries to calm us down. "You think you can book her, Jett?"

I stand up, ready to leave. "Yeah, I'll book her." Even though she's putting energy into avoiding me, I'll amp up my efforts and get her to cave. "I'll catch you guys later," I say and head out. Although we're on a break, we're working on our next album when we can catch time together and we've got plans to record later this afternoon.

As I make my way to my car, I pull out my phone and call Presley. She answers me almost straight away. "You just don't give up, do you?" I like the playfulness in her tone. It hits me right in the dick, and I decide then and there that I won't be taking no for an answer today.

"No. I'm taking you out for lunch today," I say as I get in my Jeep.

"Umm, since when?"

"Since now."

She goes quiet and then sighs. "Jett, you need to move on and find someone else. We have nothing in common."

"Bullshit."

"Okay, tell me what you love to do when you're not making music."

"Anything outdoor. Jet skiing, surfing, skydiving, camping."

"I hate the outdoors."

"What do you love to do?"

"Well, obviously photography, writing, art, going to the movies."

"I like going to the movies. What kinds of movies do you like?" I'm enjoying this conversation, and I settle back into my seat.

"Romantic comedies, thrillers, and dramas. You?"

"Action but I can do thrillers, too."

"See, nothing in common."

I try to find something else. "What kinds of holidays do you like to take?"

"The kind where I can sit by the pool or beach and drink cocktails. Maybe read a book. Let me guess, you love full-on holidays where you never stop."

"I do, but fuck, it doesn't mean we can't go on a date and see where it leads."

"Why bother starting something we know isn't going to go anywhere?"

"Bloody hell, Presley, are you always this pessimistic?"

"No, just practical. We're both busy people and neither of us have the time to put into this."

I make a decision and turn the keys in the ignition. "You'd be surprised what I have the time for, sweetheart."

"I've gotta go, Jett."

"We'll talk soon," I say, and end the call.

I immediately dial another number. Presley's got no idea what she's in for.

***

Forty minutes later, I park my car outside her apartment. She lives in Kangaroo Point, not far from where my apartment in the city is.

It's a gorgeous area, close to the river. I exit the car and squint in the sun. It's hot in Brisbane today, just the way I love it. I reach for the coffee I bought her and head up to her apartment. I'm wondering if she'll buzz me in the front door, but as I arrive at it, someone is leaving and he lets me in before the door shuts behind me. *Too easy, meant to be.*

I take the lift up to her floor, and a couple of moments later, I knock on her door.

She answers it and surprise covers her face. "Jett. What are you doing here?" She sounds unsure of herself, and I know I've made the right decision. Presley wants me as much as I want her.

I hold out her coffee, and she takes it with hesitation.

"Hazelnut with a shot of vanilla. I believe it's your favourite," I say.

"How the hell did you know that?"

I shrug. "I have my ways." I take a step forward, trying to push my way inside. She steps aside and lets me. I thank the universe for coffee that makes her momentarily forget she doesn't want to date me.

Her home is beautiful. I'd been too distracted the other night to pay much attention, but I take it all in now. Splashes of colour everywhere, plants dotted throughout and books on every spare surface. It's got that feeling my mum and dad's home has, and I'm drawn to it. After a decade of living out of a suitcase, I'd love to come home to a place like this, instead of the bland apartment I own.

"Michael told you," she accuses, and I can tell from her tone he will get his ass kicked for this.

"Yes."

"What did you offer him for that? Michael wouldn't give me up without something significant."

I grin at her. "I promised him a lucrative job for his client."

She's a clever woman and knows exactly what I'm talking about. "You bribed him with something his client isn't even interested in?"

"How was I to know his client wouldn't be interested in a job?"

She drinks some of her coffee and then returns my grin. "You're a sneaky bastard, aren't you, Jett Vaughn?"

I throw my head back and laugh. Thank fuck. *This* is the Presley I wanted to see. "I've been called worse, sweetheart."

She looks thoughtful. "And what if his client had actually agreed? How were you going to get out of that?"

"Well, considering I'm hoping to convince his client to take that job on, I wouldn't have any problems if she agreed."

She sucks in a breath. She hadn't been expecting that.

I keep talking. "I'm taking you out for lunch today."

"Oh, really?" She's putting on a good show, but I've worked her out. She wants me, but she's trying to convince herself she doesn't. All I need to do is give her a reason to let me in. I need to show her that all her reasons for not wanting me aren't important.

"Yeah, beautiful, really. I've got a booking for us in forty minutes. Can you be ready by then?"

Panic spreads across her face. "Shit, Jett. I don't know any woman who could be ready in that short amount of time. You'll need to call and push it later."

I nod. "Sure."

I can tell she's mentally flipping through her wardrobe. She points to her balcony and says, "You can sit in the sun if you want, or in here if you want. Up to you."

"Go get ready. Don't worry about me."

She hurries into her bedroom, and I head outside. I call my friend, Ernesto, who owns my favourite Italian restaurant. "How did it go?" he asks as he answers me.

I chuckle. "I told her I had a booking in forty minutes. She freaked. Told you it would work. Women forget what they want when they're all freaked like that. Made her forget she didn't want to go out with me."

"Jesus Christ, you're devious," he mutters. "I'll see you when you get here."

I thank him and hang up. He's right; I am devious, but I've never had to use my skills on a woman before. The chase is both exhilarating and frustrating. And I wonder how long it's going to take me to convince Presley to give me a shot.

CRAVE

Chapter Eight
Presley

I follow Jett into the little Italian restaurant. How the hell he managed to convince me to come with him is beyond me. He's got some sort of special powers, I'm sure of it. All he's gotta do is grace me with that sexy goddamn smile of his, and I'm like a bloody schoolgirl all over again. Falling at his fucking feet.

We're escorted to our table and place our orders. Then he says, *"Crazy Stupid Love."*

"Have you finally lost your mind?" I ask, having no clue what he means.

"*This Means War, Killers* . . . romantic comedies I like."

"Oh."

"A cruise."

"Huh?"

"A cruise would be a good holiday. You could mix it up with drinks by the pool and exploring the places the ship visits. Perfect combination, don't you think?"

My stomach does somersaults. He's put thought into this, and I have to admit I'm impressed. "Yes, I'd love to do a cruise one day," I say, softly.

He smiles and leans his elbows on the table. "Now, tell me something about you that no one knows."

I frown. "Why?"

He shrugs. "It's the kind of shit I like to know about people. It tells me something about them."

Maybe I've judged him wrong. The fact he wants to know this tells me something about *him.* "I almost got married when I was eighteen to a man twenty years older than me."

Intrigue lights his face. "What stopped you?"

"We decided on the spur of the moment to do it, but we didn't have the necessary paperwork filled out. A couple of days later, I freaked and realised I didn't really want to marry him."

"And you've never told anyone that?"

"No. Now it's your turn."

"A woman I slept with five years ago fell pregnant. I didn't think I wanted the baby but was fully prepared to support her. But just before she was three months pregnant, she aborted the baby. I was surprised at how much it upset me."

The mood between us has turned from playful and flirty to serious. I'm amazed he would tell me something so personal. Something no one else knows. "It's funny how life turns out sometimes, isn't it?" I murmur.

His smile is gentle, beautiful. "I believe things are meant to be. I'm yet to work out why that happened the way it did, but I know one day it'll be made clear."

The more he talks, the more he affects me. The more I want to open myself up to him. "I believe that, too."

"So, we do have something in common."

"It would seem we do," I agree, giving him a smile in return.

"Well, thank fuck for that."

I have to laugh. And I have to give him credit for the time he's put into chasing me.

"So, tell me about your band," I say, half out of interest, half out of a desire to let him convince me to take a chance on him.

"We've been together for ten years. I put a call out for band members when I was eighteen, and they were the dickheads who answered it. It took us about five years to really get our name out there and then we cracked the US market. Haven't looked back."

"I'm gathering you're a pretty big international band, right?"

"Yeah."

"How the hell can you get away with the stuff you do then?"

Confusion flickers in his eyes. "What stuff?"

I throw my arms out to the side. "This kind of stuff. We've been out a few times, and no one's bothered you. If I didn't know better, I wouldn't think you were a famous rocker."

"Sweetheart, there's security outside. I've always got them with me. You just don't see them. They not only keep me safe, they keep the fans away," he explains, making perfect sense. I should have realised he'd have security.

Our food arrives and we continue to trade stories about our lives. Jett continues to surprise me by revealing a man I'm impressed with.

"So, I know your parents are still together but do you have any brothers or sisters?" he asks.

"I've got an older brother, Stuart. We're pretty close, but he lives overseas for work so I don't see him very often."

"What does he do?"

"He's an actor and is trying to break into movies in the States. He's been there for four years with no luck yet, but he's determined so I hope that pays off soon. How about you? Any siblings?"

He nods. "Yeah, a younger sister, Claudia. She's still living at home with Mum and Dad while she finishes studying to be a nurse. I try to keep an eye on her because she has this tendency to get mixed up with the wrong guys."

"Ah, that must be hard for you to watch as the older brother."

"Like you wouldn't fucking believe," he mutters. It's clear to me he loves his family very much, and I love that about him.

We finish our mains, and as we continue to chat over dessert, I stop him to confirm something he just told me. "Wait, you sponsor ten children in Indonesia?"

"Yeah," he says like it's the most natural thing to do in life.

"That's awesome."

"We met them a couple of years ago."

"Who is 'we'?"

"Me and the boys. They've sponsored kids over there, too. But a couple of years ago we went over and helped build houses. I've gotta say, it was one of the best experiences I've ever had." His enthusiasm is infectious. Hell, if they hired Jett to promote those programs, they'd probably get a huge increase in people signing up to help.

"Fuck," I mutter.

"What?" I've totally confused him.

"You make it bloody hard for a woman to not want to date you," I gripe.

112

He bursts out laughing. "Presley, has anyone ever told you how fucking sexy you are when you grumble like that?"

"No. Most men hate it."

"Well, I like it, so don't change, okay?"

Happiness flows through me at his words, and I'm sure I take the last step towards the edge of allowing Jett in. And by the time we finish our meal, I'm completely captivated by him and under his spell. I know I'll probably give him whatever he wants now.

***

The next morning, I say goodbye to Jett at my front door and then head back inside. He stayed over last night and gave me another reason why I should date him. The man has mad skills in the bedroom, and I'm looking forward to seeing him again.

I shower and get ready for the day. I've got a full day ahead of me, editing more photos from the Crave concert shoot. As I sit down to get started, there's a knock at my front door. A minute later, my happy bubble bursts when I find my husband standing on the other side of the door.

"Presley," he says while taking a step inside.

I put my arm up to block him, and he comes to a halt, clearly stunned I would deny him access.

"No, Lennon, you don't get to come inside. What do you want?"

"I told you I was coming home," he says as if that answers my question.

"*This* isn't your home. Not anymore."

"My name is still on the deed."

"Oh my god! That means jack shit, asshole. You walked out, so it's not your home."

"I made a mistake, Presley."

"Yeah, you did, but it corrected the mistake I made when I married you, so let's call it even."

"I want to come home, baby." His voice has that soft tone he uses when he wants something from me, but it won't work anymore. A year ago, I would have given him anything he wanted when he spoke to me this way. I've since learnt my lesson.

"No. And don't call me that anymore."

His face tells me he wasn't expecting this. He must have expected me to roll over and give him whatever he wanted, just like everyone else in his life does. "I'll give you the baby you always wanted." He promises me the one thing that came between us the most when we were together.

Anger mixes with pain, and I'm done. "Fuck you, Lennon. You can't worm your way back into my life with shit like that. Yeah, I wanted a baby with you, but *you* never wanted that, so don't come here now and make bullshit promises to get what you want in return. I don't want a baby with you anymore." I spit my words at him and then move to close the door in his face.

He puts a foot inside to stop the door from closing. "I'm not giving up on us, Presley," he promises, and I see the determination on his face. Shit, he means this, and when Lennon wants something, he does everything to get it. I do *not* need this in my life. Not when I've finally decided to start something with Jett.

"Goodbye," I say and shove his foot out of the way so I can slam the door shut. Once I have the door closed, I sag against it.

Shit.

I hope he gives up, but I know he won't. Not until he's exhausted all avenues.

Fuck.

***

I look at the room I've just stepped into. It's a fundraising event for breast cancer research, and it's decorated in pink and white. They've pulled out all the stops with balloons, flowers, candles, and pretty party lights everywhere. It's like a magical wonderland, and I stare in awe. I wish I had my camera with me; I could get some amazing photos of all this.

Jett pulls me close and murmurs against my ear, "Thank you for coming tonight."

He called me four hours ago and asked me to come. I didn't hesitate to say yes. Smiling at him, I say, "Any excuse to wear a party dress."

"I'll remember that," he promises while scanning the room. His gaze settles on the bar. "I'm gonna go get some drinks. What would you like?"

"Surprise me with a cocktail."

He nods. "Will do. You'll be right at the table with the boys?"

"Absolutely. I'm looking forward to hanging out with them tonight."

"Good. They're looking forward to it, too."

"Really?"

"Yes, really. They like you. Told me not to fuck it up."

I turn to face him and loop my hands around his neck. He bends to give me a quick kiss, and when we pull apart, I say, "I'm so happy I decided to go on a date with you, Jett Vaughn."

"Me too, sweetheart. You've no idea just how happy."

I like his honesty, and the fact he doesn't hesitate to make himself vulnerable to me.

"Okay, go. If you get enough cocktails in me tonight, you might get your way with me later."

"Really? I think your sex addiction would guarantee me that without cocktails."

"Yeah, yeah," I mutter. He's totally right. I shove him gently. "Go."

He gives me one last sexy grin and then leaves. I admire him as he walks away. Jett's wearing a suit tonight and looks so hot I'm sure we'll have to leave early so I can satisfy my addiction.

"Presley!"

I turn to find West motioning for me to join the rest of the band at the table. I'm surprised none of them brought a date tonight. I'm the only woman in the group. I make my way over to them and take a seat.

"Looking good, babe," West says, his eyes gazing appreciatively at my body for a moment. I'm wearing a fitted, floor-length black evening dress, that has gorgeous beading over the thin straps and a long slit that ends mid thigh. Jett's eyes almost bulged out of his head when he picked me up.

"Fuck, West, don't. The last thing we need is Jett losing his shit tonight," Hunter warns him.

I eye West. "Thank you for the compliment but I think Hunter's right. Let's not rile Jett up tonight."

"I know I've said it before, but I fucking like you, Presley. You say it like it is," West says.

Van's been lounging in his chair, an angry glare fixed on his face. But he looks at me now and asks, "Has Jett convinced you to photograph our next tour yet?"

"We haven't really discussed it."

"You should consider it. Your photography is fucking amazing. We'd be lucky to have you." It's the nicest he's been to me so far, and I'm floored by his kind words.

"Thank you," I say to him, and he nods and then goes back to his angry glaring. I'm thinking Van's a man of little words.

I chat with West and Hunter for another couple of minutes before excusing myself to go to the ladies' room. When I arrive there, the line is five deep, and I kill time by texting Erin.

Me: At charity event with Jett. You should see him in a suit...

Erin: Shut it. Don't tell me any more bitch.

Me: LOL

Erin: You heard from your asshole husband again?

Me: Not since he showed at my door two days ago.

Erin: Good. Sorry, gotta go chick. Talk to you later xx

Me: Night xx

I finally reach the end of the line, and five minutes later, I'm heading back out to the

119

table. The sight I'm greeted with when I get there takes me aback. Lennon's here and he and Van are going head to head over something. Both men are furious about whatever it is.

"You wouldn't know the meaning of fucking loyalty," Van spits at Lennon.

"She told me you two were over. How the fuck was I to know she was lying?"

"It's called friendship, motherfucker. We were friends, and you don't do that to a friend. You don't fuck his fiancée behind his fucking back."

"Do you fucking listen, Van? I didn't know you were still together."

"Yeah, well, it's not good enough. You should have asked me, not her. She wasn't your fucking friend, *I* was."

Jett steps in to try and break them apart because they look like they're at the point where fists could start flying any minute. "Van, leave it. He's not fucking worth it."

Van's eyes are wild when he looks at Jett. "I told you coming tonight was a bad fucking idea."

Jett directs his attention to Lennon. "You need to leave. Now."

Lennon shifts his gaze and stops when he sees me. "Presley? What the hell are you doing here?"

Jett swings around to look between Lennon and me. "You know this asshole?" he demands.

"Yes."

Before I can explain myself further, Lennon says, "She's my wife, asshole. Get your fucking eyes off her."

Jett looks like he's about to explode with anger. "What the fuck?" he roars at no one in particular, and I'm not sure if he's directing that at Lennon or me.

Shit, this is a clusterfuck.

"I *was* your wife," I correct Lennon.

"You still are," Lennon says.

"On paper only. Give me six months, and I'll rectify that."

Jett interrupts us. Looking at Lennon, he says, "Like I said, you need to fucking leave."

I nod in agreement and Lennon assesses the situation for a moment before finally doing what Jett suggested.

Van glares at him until he can't see him anymore and then he says, "Fuck it, Jett, I'm out. Sorry man, but I can't be in the same room as him or I will fucking punch him, and that's the last thing we need." His face is a mask of anger and apology.

Jett nods. "Yeah, you're right. You should go."

Van doesn't wait around and a moment later he's gone, and I'm left with Jett staring at me. He's still angry but there's a calmness to it now. "You're married to Lennon?" He's incredulous and I don't blame him. I haven't mentioned my marriage at all.

"Yes."

"Why didn't you tell me?"

"We split up six months ago, and I'm done with him. I'm just waiting for the year to be up so I can file for divorce. I don't consider myself married anymore."

His chest heaves and he seems relieved with that answer. "Thank fuck."

I move to where he is and lay a hand on his chest. "I promise there's nothing left there," I say softly.

He grabs my waist and pulls me into his space. "I believe you, sweetheart. I'm more surprised by the fact I've known Lennon for years but I've not once met you. I knew he was married but never knew who to. How the fuck did you guys work it that way? If you were my wife, I wouldn't let you out of my sight."

"He didn't want me on tour with him and because I was busy with my work, he had no trouble selling that to me. It hurt, though." My voice cracks on my last few words, and Jett wraps me in his arms.

"Fuck," he mutters. "He's an asshole, baby. You're better off without him."

"I know," I mumble into his body. "But he's told me he'll do anything to get me back, and when Lennon wants something, he'll do anything to get it."

Jett lets me go enough to look down into my eyes. There's a fierce determination in his. "So will I, Presley, and I want you. If Lennon thinks he can come back and pick up where he left off, he can fucking think again. You're mine now, not his."

I suck in a breath.

This could get messy.

Really fucking messy.

Be The One (Crave #2) Coming Soon

Acknowledgements

I'd like to thank the authors I worked with on the Owned Anthology that All Your Reasons was written for. Jani Kay, thanks for being you and suggesting this idea in the first place. Without you, this wouldn't even be happening. I've loved working with all the authors on this anthology but I do need to give a shout out to Lyra for doing the formatting – you rock!! And Lilliana for all your time designing the website and graphics . . . sometimes more than once! Nothing was ever a trouble for either of you ladies and I am so very thankful for the time you put in.

To my beta readers – Melanie, Christina, Paula, Amanda & Becca – thank you so much ladies! Your feedback was invaluable and I truly appreciate the time you gave me to do it.

To Jenny at Editing 4 Indies. Wow, this is the first time we've worked together and I need to say a HUGE thank you for doing it at the last minute for me. You made the process so easy and I am very thankful.

To my friends and family - thank you for being patient with me while I have ignored you to get this book done. I love you.

To my PA and friend, Melanie Sassymum, thank you for everything you do for me. You help keep me sane in the madness of it all, babe. I love you for it all.

To Letitia, my amazing cover designer! Thank you so much for designing me a cover that I loved from the very first second I saw it. Working with you has been effortless, and I thank you so much for making my life easier by taking control of this. At a time when I was knee deep in both professional and personal things, and trying to get a book ready for release, you came along and were a breath of fresh air. You probably don't realise just what you did for me and how very grateful I am for you. Thank you xx

To all bloggers, thank you so very much for everything you do to help me. You ladies have hearts of gold!

To my Stormchasers. I hope you love Jett as much as you love our bikers! He doesn't have the asshole in him that they do but I kinda love that about him. Thank you for all your support, encouragement and most importantly, your friendship. I would be lost without you, ladies!

To my readers! Thank you for reading my books and I hope you loved Jett as much as I do.

About The Author

Nina Levine is an Aussie writer who writes stories about alpha men and the strong, independent women they love.

When she isn't creating with words, she loves to create with paint and paper. Often though, she can be found curled up with a good book and some chocolate.

Visit Nina here: www.ninalevinebooks.com

Also by Nina Levine

USA Today & International Bestselling Author

Storm MC Series
Storm (Storm MC #1)
Fierce (Storm MC #2)
Blaze (Storm MC #2.5)
Revive (Storm MC #3)
Slay (Storm MC #4)
Illusive (Storm MC #5) – COMING 2015
Command (Storm MC #6) – COMING 2015

Sydney Storm MC Series
Relent (Sydney Storm MC #1)

Havoc Series
Destined Havoc (Havoc #1)
Inevitable Havoc (Havoc #2) – COMING 2015

Crave Series
All Your Reasons (Crave #1)
Be The One (Crave #2) – COMING 2015

Made in the USA
Charleston, SC
05 April 2015